DAPHNE AND THE

BIGGEST EGG IN THE

WORLD

By E. F. JENKINS

ISBN : 978 1500446499

Pictures by Elaine Frances Jenkins

This little story is dedicated to my mother Anne who taught me loving kindness and to my wonderful husband Neil who taught me perseverance.

Thank you and I hope you enjoy this little story.

CHAPTER 1

One day Daphne was sitting by the river bank daydreaming, when suddenly, the biggest egg Daphne had ever seen came rolling down towards her.

"Oh stop, stop," cried a frightened Daphne.

To Daphne's relief and surprise the huge egg stopped right in front of her little webbed feet.

Still feeling a little afraid, Daphne quacked "Egg you are so…. Big !"

"Where did you come from ?"

Daphne spoke again. "Are you lost?"

"I know, I will try and keep you warm until your mummy finds you."

So Daphne clambered carefully on top of the biggest egg she had ever seen.

Just then, Old Hilary Hen was passing by. "Oh my, oh my, my dear Daphne, however did you lay that ?" clucked Old Hilary Hen.

"No, Hilary Hen, it`s not my egg, I`m just looking after it for someone."

"For whom ?" clucked Old Hilary Hen in her most superior voice.

Then Daphne thought for a moment.
"I don`t know, well not yet."

Old Hilary Hen looked down her
beak at Daphne and said :-

"Daphne, I think you will find, in time, that this is NOT an EGG but a LARGE WHITE STONE !"

Then Old Hilary Hen wandered away with her head in the air.

Daphne felt hurt.

"You are not a stone! You are the BIGGEST EGG IN THE WORLD and I am going to stay with you and keep you warm until your mummy finds you," she said.

Daphne stretched her little brown wings over the Biggest Egg in the World to keep as much of it as warm as she could.

CHAPTER 2

It wasn`t long before Suzie Seagull came down from high in the sky.

"I`ve been watching you for AGES from up here," said Suzie Seagull. "Are you alright, or are you STUCK ?" squawked Suzie seagull.

"No, I`m not stuck ! I am nesting on THE BIGGEST EGG IN THE WORLD."

"Don`t be silly, that`s not an egg, it`s a BALL. I see them all the time on my travels, in PARKS, in FIELDS, on BEACHES, in BACK GARDENS."

"Oh Daphne, how silly you are !" and with a shriek of laughter, Suzie Seagull flew away.

Daphne felt hurt.

"You really are the BIGGEST EGG IN THE WORLD and I am going to look after you until your mummy finds you," she said, giving the egg the

biggest cuddle she could with her
little brown wings.

CHAPTER 3

Now Daphne was feeling happier.

The sun was high in the sky and it was a very hot and sunny day.

Daphne needed to cool down and she was feeling hungry, so she gently slid off the Biggest Egg in the World and waddled into the river.

"I won`t be long," she promised.

On the other side of the river was Russell the River Rat. He stood up on his hind legs and watched as Daphne slipped into the river.

Seeing his chance, he scurried over to the other side and when he got to the egg he tried to bite it with his sharp yellow teeth.

Tap-tap, tap-tap, tap-tap. Russell kept trying to break into the egg.

On hearing the tapping, Daphne looked up. With horror, she yelled :-

"Stop it, stop it ! Get off, get off Russell," she yelled as she raced out of the water as fast as her little wings and webbed feet would carry her.

"Hey, cool down there duck, what's the fuss ?" said Russell the River Rat, leaning against the Biggest Egg in the World.

"This is the Biggest Egg in the World and you nearly cracked it" quacked a VERY cross and wet Daphne.

"Not so fast my feathered friend, this ain't no egg ! If it was, I would have broken into it by now!

"Daphne you dozy duck, it`s a hard hat !

I see them all the time on men`s heads when they`re building things," as he tried to push the Biggest Egg in the World closer to the river.

"I thought I would sail it down the river for the day seeing as you`ve had it all morning. It`s my turn to have a go."

"Oh, stop it at once," yelled Daphne, getting more angry than she`d ever been.

"This is an egg and I`m keeping it safe until its` mummy comes back."

"You can`t be serious," said Russell the River Rat. "I know you`re not the sharpest tool in the box but you don`t really believe this is an egg do you ?"

Before Daphne could answer, Russell the River Rat started to laugh. He laughed and he laughed. He laughed so much that he clutched his tummy and rolled himself up into a ball, and rolled away.

CHAPTER 4

Daphne stroked the egg.

"I`m so sorry, Egg. I thought you`d be safe. I won`t leave you again."

She carefully climbed up onto the Biggest Egg in the World and spread her little brown wings over it and gave it a big hug.

Daphne sat on the Biggest Egg in the World and waited and waited and waited, dozing in the warm sun, when suddenly the ground began to tremble and the egg rocked.

"Help" quacked Daphne." What`s happening ?"

As Daphne looked up she saw the strangest thing she had ever seen. She wanted to fly away, she wanted to scream, but instead, Daphne just froze. Striding towards her was an ENORMOUS bird. It was the scariest thing Daphne had ever seen.

She put her little brown wings over her eyes hoping she wouldn`t be seen.

Then this bird with the longest, hairiest legs she`d ever seen stopped right next to her.

"Thank you for looking after my Egg, she rolled away this morning. I`ve been looking everywhere for her ."

Daphne summoned up all her courage and in a very small voice said, "excuse me, I`m Daphne, but what and who are you ?"

"Oh, how rude of me. My name is Ophelia the Ostrich. You can call me Ophelia. You have MY Egg ! I see that you have been keeping her warm and safe. Thank you my little friend."

Just then, Suzie Seagull flew overhead. When she saw Ophelia the Ostrich next to Daphne and the Egg, she squawked so loudly she dropped her dinner.

CHAPTER 5

Old Hilary Hen was returning from her day out and when she saw Ophelia the Ostrich she clucked and clucked in panic.

"Oh my, oh my, oh my", she said and hurried away to hide.

"It`s alright, Hilary" said Daphne, but Old Hilary Hen was too frightened to stop and listen.

It wasn`t long before Ophelia and Daphne heard Russell the River Rat singing. He was throwing stones at an old can. Daphne called out to Russell.

"Russell, Russell, have you met Ophelia the Ostrich ?"

"Stone the crows, that`s one BIG BIRD !", he said as he fell back on his bottom.

"Yes, I suppose I am," said Ophelia in her deep grand voice. "My friend

Daphne has been keeping my lost Egg warm and safe whilst I have been looking everywhere for her."

Russell looked at Daphne "Well, you did tell me it was a big Egg, didn`t you. You are one smart duck Daphne."

Then Russell the River Rat leaned over to the Biggest Egg in the World and whispered "sorry for trying to bite you."

Daphne looked at Ophelia and they started to laugh, when .....

The Biggest Egg in the World started to move from side to side. Then, a tiny tapping could be heard coming from inside the Egg, then another tap and another tap, tap, tap.

Daphne slid off the Egg just in time as the Biggest Egg in the World cracked right down the middle.

Daphne and Ophelia held their breath as out popped a beautiful fluffy chick.

"OLIVIA my love, I`ve been waiting for you," cried Ophelia.

As she stretched out her HUGE wing and gathered up her perfect little chick, there was another tiny little chirp coming from inside the broken shell.

Daphne stepped closer and pecked off a piece of the broken shell.

"Chirp , chirp , MUM is that you ?"

"YES my little DORIS, it`s me." said a very proud Daphne.

Daphne saw the most beautiful little chick she had ever seen and as Ophelia had done, Daphne gathered tiny Doris safely under her soft warm brown wings and gave her a big cuddle.

THE END

NOW COLOUR YOUR FAVOURITE CHARACTERS

DAPHNE

THE EGG

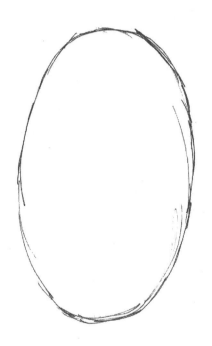

OLD HILARY HEN

SUZIE SEAGULL

RUSSELL RAT

OPHELIA THE OSTRICH

OLIVIA OSTRICH

DORIS DUCK

Made in the USA
Charleston, SC
16 October 2014